Renoir and the Boy with the Long Hair

A story about Pierre-Auguste Renoir

by Wendy Wax

Illustrated by Nancy Lane

"What a pretty girl," says a woman. She is pointing to a painting by Pierre-Auguste Renoir at a gallery show by the famous artist. Renoir's vibrant, colorful paintings light up the room and bring joy to the admiring crowd.

"That's *not* a girl. It's a boy," says a man. This man happens to be Jean Renoir, the son of the artist and the subject of *Jean Renoir Sewing*, the painting in front of them.

"But his hair is so long!" says the woman.

As the woman moves on to the next painting, Jean's cousin Gabrielle laughs. "You used to hate being teased about your long hair," she says.

"If only my stubborn father had let me get a haircut," Jean says with a smile.

They remember back to those days in the sunny South of France . . .

Young Jean and his teenage cousin Gabrielle, who he called Bee-bon, were walking to the market. Gabrielle had come to live with the Renoirs to help out during Jean's birth and to care for him afterward.

Suddenly, Jean dove behind Gabrielle. "What are you doing?" she asked.

"Hiding from the washerwoman," said Jean. "I hate when she calls me 'pretty.'"

"Well, you can come out of hiding now," Gabrielle informed him. "The milkman is going over to talk to her."

Jean returned to Gabrielle's side—just as a group of neighborhood boys surrounded them.

"Hey, girl!" a boy teased Jean. "Where's your skirt?"

"I'm not a girl," said Jean, blushing a deep red.

"He's a wolf-head," snickered another boy.

"I am not," shouted Jean. How dare that boy associate him with the bushy end of a ceiling mop!

"Don't you boys have anything better to do?" asked Gabrielle.

Feeling foolish, the boys scattered, and Jean and Gabrielle continued on their way.

On their way home, they saw Renoir painting a tree. He was observing the movement of a branch so closely he didn't notice the small crowd forming around him.

"I'm going to ask him if I can get a haircut," said Jean.

"Not now!" said Gabrielle. "You know your father doesn't like to be disturbed while he paints."

"That artist sure wears strange clothes," said a young girl in the crowd.

"And a silly hat," said her brother.

Jean admired his father for not caring what others thought of him. He wished he were more like that.

6

Suddenly, a cloud blocked the sun, and
Renoir looked up from his canvas.

"Jean! Gabrielle! I'm glad you're
here!" he called happily, as the crowd
admired his painting of women lounging in the shade.

"That painting is too pretty to be art," said a man.

"Why *shouldn't* art be pretty?" said Renoir. "There are enough unpleasant
things in the world. I try to capture the joy of life in my paintings."

Just then, the sun reappeared. With a wink and a wave, Renoir got back
to work. Jean would have to wait till later to ask for a haircut.

7

Before dinner, Jean found Renoir in the kitchen sketching his wife.

"Can I get my hair cut?" he asked. "The other boys call me 'girl' and 'wolf-head.'"

"Girls are pretty," Renoir said thoughtfully, "but wolf-heads? This I have a problem with." Renoir disliked these ceiling mops because people used them to kill his spider friends.

"Please, Papa," Jean pleaded.

"Absolutely not!" said Renoir. "Your long hair will protect you from the sun's rays, and cushion you if you fall. Your brother Pierre didn't have his hair cut until he went to school, and neither will you."

Feeling defeated, Jean went to wash his hands for dinner.

After dinner, Jean visited his pet rabbit, Jeannot, in the dining room. "I'm tired of being the boy with long hair," he told the rabbit.

Having overheard, Gabrielle suggested they take the rabbit for a walk.

"Bee-bon," said Jean as they climbed a hill. "I'll be starting school soon, won't I?"

"Not too soon," Gabrielle said, putting her arm around him. "Your father is in no rush to send you. He believes children learn more from being outdoors than being stuck in a classroom."

Jean sighed. "Well he can't keep me out of school forever."

On Saturday nights, the Renoirs often had friends over for dinner. Many were artists, art dealers, and models, and the conversation was always lively.

Jean liked to listen to Renoir and his artist friends talk about the old days when they left their dark studios to paint in the open air. Renoir and his friends Claude Monet, Alfred Sisley, and Frederic Bazille often met in cafés to discuss new ideas about painting. Then they went into the forest to experiment using brighter colors and quicker brush strokes than they'd ever used before.

"I once spent an entire day studying the way the sunlight changed on a leaf," Renoir remembered.

"You were the only one of us who loved using black," remembered Monet. "The rest of us used only bright colors."

"You became known as Impressionists," said Jean, who had heard the story many times before.

During dessert one evening, Renoir's friend Paul Cezanne asked Jean how long he planned to grow his hair.

"I want it cut, but Papa won't let me," Jean complained. "He says it protects my head."

Cezanne chuckled. "I bet the real reason is because he likes to paint the play of light in your shiny, golden hair," he said.

Before Jean could respond, a voice at the other end of the table grew louder. It was an art dealer scolding Renoir for giving away paintings to anyone who asked—they were worth a lot of money!

At one time, Renoir's Impressionist paintings had hardly been worth a cent! Some people thought they were blurry. Others thought he was nuts for painting in such a sloppy style.

When people finally started to appreciate Impressionism, Renoir changed his style once again.

He combined Impressionism . . .
(*Bal du Moulin de la Galette*)

with his old style of painting . . .
(*Lise with Sunshade*)

and came up with a mixture of both (*The Umbrellas*).

The Renoirs spent most winters in Paris and summers in the country.

"Papa, why do we have to move so much?" Jean asked, as they rode the train to Paris. His feet were rested on his suitcase, and his pet lizard was nestled in his pocket.

"Every time we move, I get a chance to paint a new kind of light," explained Renoir.

"Every time we move," said Jean, "I get teased by a new group of boys."

Just then, a lady entered the compartment and sat across from them. "What a sweet girl!" she exclaimed when she saw Jean. "Such pretty hair!"

While Jean turned as red as his suitcase, the lizard poked its head out of his pocket.

"Ahhhh!" shrieked the lady, and she hurried out of the compartment.

Jean and his family laughed until the lady returned with a guard who threw Jean's lizard out the window and left.

"That's not fair!" cried Jean, seething with anger. The thought of his poor lizard flying through the air left him brokenhearted.

"Look on the bright side," Renoir said kindly. "Your lizard is back in nature where he belongs. Imagine him landing in a field of his lizard friends."

Jean did this—but it made him feel only a little better.

One morning Jean found Renoir hanging his paintings in the front hall, which he did
each time they moved. Being surrounded by his father's paintings made Jean feel at
home no matter where they lived.

Jean was about to offer to help when they heard a knock. Renoir opened the door.

"Hello! Come in!" Renoir said, ushering a couple into the front hall. They had
come to welcome the Renoirs to the neighborhood.

"These paintings are wonderful!" exclaimed the woman.

"This one would look perfect in our parlor."

"Take it!" said Renoir. "It's yours!"

"But Papa, the art dealer said not to . . ." Jean began—but Renoir was already taking the painting down. He was always giving his paintings away no matter what they were worth. He was just too nice.

19

One sunny morning, Jean raced to the door. "I want to go outside," he said to Gabrielle and Renoir, who were still at the breakfast table.

"Real gold," said Renoir.

"What?" said Jean.

"Your hair shines like gold in the sunlight," Renoir said dreamily. "Let's go up to my studio so I can paint you. The light is perfect."

"But I . . . I . . . have a sore leg . . . and sitting in one place will make it worse," Jean said. He began to limp around the table.

"Is that true?" asked Renoir, winking at Gabrielle.

"No," said Jean, sorry about the lie.

"I know!" said Gabrielle. "You can sew a coat for your tin camel while your father paints you. Winter is coming and he's going to need to stay warm."

Jean thought for a moment. The tin camel was his favorite toy, and he really did want it to stay warm. "Well . . . okay," he said, a bit reluctantly, and followed his father and Gabrielle upstairs.

Renoir kept his studio neat and clean. Gabrielle and his wife were the only ones allowed to touch his brushes and palette.

While Renoir mixed colors, Gabrielle found a piece of satin for the camel's coat. She helped Jean thread the needle, and he got right to work. He barely even noticed when Renoir tied a yellow ribbon in his hair!

Jean sat still for hours, sewing and listening to the sound of Renoir's humming and quick brush strokes. Renoir and Gabrielle were amazed! Usually Gabrielle had to read fairy tales to keep Jean still. Renoir loved hearing the fairy tales as much as Jean did—especially "Soup from a Sausage Skewer."

Deep in concentration, Renoir didn't just paint his son from the outside. He felt as if he could see Jean on the inside, too, and painted him as if he were doing his own portrait. This is the way Renoir painted every portrait, whether he was being paid by a wealthy patron or painting for pure delight.

"It's one of your best," said Jean's mother,
when *Jean Renoir Sewing* was finally finished. Gabrielle agreed.

"What do you think, Jean?" asked Renoir.

"I think I look like a girl," said Jean. "Please, Papa, can you send me to
school so I can get my hair cut?"

"Not until you're ten," said Renoir.

"Ten!" exclaimed Jean, his mother, and Gabrielle at the same time. But
they knew it was senseless to argue.

Jean's hair grew longer and longer. A year passed, then another. When he turned seven, his little brother Claude, who they called Coco, was born.

"I feel so big next to him," Jean said, as Coco grasped his finger.

"Big enough to go to school?" asked Renoir.

Jean looked up with curiosity. "Yes, Papa. But I'm not ten yet," he said.

With a twinkle in his eye, Renoir said, "I think it's time for school and a haircut." Jean was thrilled!

Jean's whole family accompanied him to the barbershop. While his mother instructed the barber, Renoir ran his fingers through Jean's hair.

As the barber began to cut, Jean's mother and Gabrielle cried. Renoir was filled with disappointment, knowing he'd never be able to paint Jean's long, reddish-gold hair again.

Jean, on the other hand, was just as happy as could be!

Jean's short hair didn't stop Renoir from painting him though. *Jean Renoir Drawing* was the first painting he did of Jean with short hair! Now that he looked like a boy, Jean was a happy model—especially when Gabrielle told his favorite fairy tale, "Soup from a Sausage Skewer," which the three of them knew by heart.

Back at the gallery, Renoir's paintings have put everyone in a cheerful mood.

"What a nice looking boy," a woman says to her husband as they stop in front of *Jean Renoir Sewing*.

"How can you tell it's a boy?" Jean asks with surprise.

"I know he is Renoir's son Jean, who became a famous movie director," says the woman. "Renoir must have passed down his creative genius. Jean Renoir's movies are fabulous!"

"Thank you," says Jean, who is proud of the movies he has made. Then he introduces himself.

"You must have made your father very proud," says the woman.

Jean smiles. "I've always been proud of him. Not only was he a great painter, he was also an amazing father."